HELPING YOUR BRAND-NEW READER

Here's how to make first-time reading easy and fun:

◗ Read the introduction at the beginning of each story aloud. Look through the pictures together so that your child can see what happens in the story before reading the words.

◗ Read the first page or so to your child, placing your finger under each word.

◗ Let your child touch the words and read the rest of the story. Give him or her time to figure out each new word.

◗ If your child gets stuck on a word, you might say, *"Try something. Look at the picture. What would make sense?"*

◗ If your child is still stuck, supply the right word. This will allow him or her to continue to read and enjoy the story. You might say, *"Could this word be 'ball'?"*

◗ Always praise your child. Praise what he or she reads correctly, and praise good tries too.

◗ Give your child lots of chances to read the story again and again. The more your child reads, the more confident he or she will become.

◗ Have fun!

First edition 2004

Library of Congress Cataloging-in-Publication Data is available.

Library of Congress Catalog Card Number 2003069716

ISBN 0-7636-2349-0

2 4 6 8 10 9 7 5 3 1

Printed in China

This book was typeset in Letraset Arta.
The illustrations were done in
watercolor and ink.

Candlewick Press
2067 Massachusetts Avenue
Cambridge, Massachusetts 02140

visit us at www.candlewick.com

Three
Little
Bears

CANDLEWICK PRESS
CAMBRIDGE, MASSACHUSETTS

David Martin ILLUSTRATED BY **Akemi Gutierrez**

Contents

OH NO, NO SHORTS!

Introduction

This story is called *Oh No, No Shorts!*
It's about how the three little bears all
have different color shorts and jump in
the water. Then Baby Bear climbs out.

Sister Bear has blue shorts.

4

Brother Bear has red shorts.

Baby Bear has green shorts.

6

Sister Bear jumps in the water.

7

Brother Bear jumps in the water.

Baby Bear jumps in the water.

Baby Bear climbs out of the water.

10

Oh no! Baby Bear has no shorts!

LICK, LICK, DRIP, DRIP

Introduction

This story is called *Lick, Lick, Drip, Drip.*
It's about how the three little bears have
ice cream. After they lick it, it starts to drip.

12

13

Brother Bear has ice cream.

14

Sister Bear has ice cream.

15

Baby Bear has ice cream.

16

Lick, lick, lick.

Brother Bear's ice cream drips.

Sister Bear's ice cream drips.

Baby Bear's ice cream drip, drip, drips.

20

Lick, lick, lick, lick, lick.

IT'S SNOWING!

Introduction

This story is called *It's Snowing!* It's about how the three little bears are happy it's snowing. They make snow bears, and then they make something else.

23

"It's snowing!" says Sister Bear.

24

"It's snowing!" says Brother Bear.

25

"It's snowing!" says Baby Bear.

26

Sister Bear makes a snow bear.

Brother Bear makes a snow bear.

Baby Bear makes a snow bear.

Then the three bears make . . .

30

snowballs!

LIMBO, LIMBO

Introduction

This story is called *Limbo, Limbo*. It's about how the three little bears play limbo. They go lower and lower until they see who can limbo the lowest.

"I can limbo," says Brother Bear.

"I can limbo," says Sister Bear.

"I can limbo," says Baby Bear.

36

"I can limbo lower," says Brother Bear.

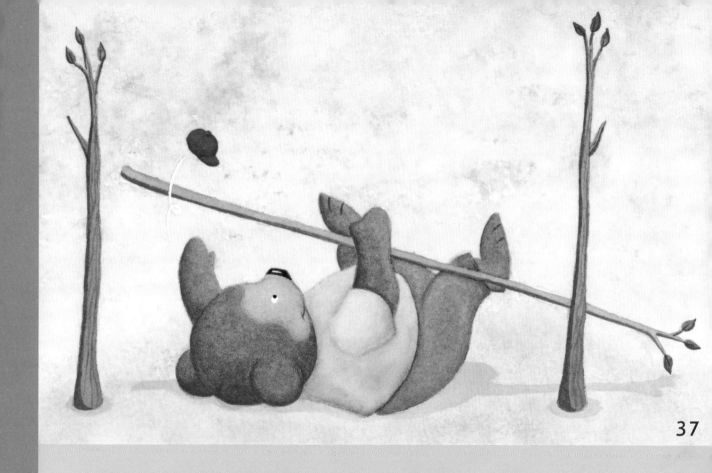

"Oops," says Brother Bear.

"I can limbo lower," says Sister Bear.

"Oops," says Sister Bear.

"I can limbo the lowest," says Baby Bear.